Dinner emergency

Sitting in my living room enjoying my luxurious apartment in Orlando, Florida. My doorbell rang and I looked at the camera feed.

I thought oh wow it's my next-door neighbor. Damn she is fine as hell in a sexy little robe. I was in a robe too, so I went to the door and opened it. She said hi I'm your next-door neighbor Rachel.

I said sure come on in, she said she had an emergency. I said how can I help. She said I'm supposed to make dinner for my husband, but my stove crapped out. I called maintenance and they said that it will take two weeks since it's a custom stove for each apartment.

I said oh wow, you can use my kitchen to make your husbands dinner. Rachel hugged me tight and said thank you so much, you are a lifesaver. She said I owe you big for this one. I smiled and said happy to help out a damsel in distress, she laughed.

I took the lovely Rachel to my kitchen. She said oh my god this is so beautiful, a chef's kitchen wow, I said its pricey, but I love it. Rachel said I bet you do.

She said I'll go get my stuff to make my husband's dinner and I'll be right back. I said cool. I left the camera on and when she was near the door. I opened up and let her in with all her stuff on a cart.

I showed her where all the stuff was in my kitchen. She started cooking and we started talking. I moved in six months ago, I told her sorry that I haven't introduced myself to you guys yet.

Rachel said its ok happy to finally meet you. I said so you're a stay-at-home wife. Rachel said yeah and what do you do. I said I'm retired from the hedge fund business, right now I just do consulting on stock and bonds when I want to.

She said cool, did I mention that I love your kitchen. I said it's all yours until you get a new stove. Rachel said thank you so much and hugged me tight. I said my pleasure, Rachel. I said your husband is a very lucky man to have such a beautiful and attentive wife. She turned red with embarrassment.

She said that is very kind of you to say. An hour later when she was finished, I helped her take it back to her apartment. When I was about to leave. She hugged me tight again with that hot body and said thanks again for letting me use your kitchen to make my husband his nightly dinner.

I said my pleasure happy to help out. The next day, I saw her at the door, and I opened it before she could press the button. I invited her in, and she hugged me tight again. I love hugging hot Rachel.

She said I'm going to make you some macadamia nut cookies for helping me out. I said great you know how I love those. She said I remember from our conversation yesterday.

Today Rachel was wearing some sexy short shorts and a tight t-shirt no bra. I could see her nipples were hard. Damn her sweet white thighs were amazing and her ass was out of this world.

Good thing that I was wearing a robe, or she would see a tent in my pants. I watched her closely as she made me cookies. When she was done, I got some milk and poured us both a glass of milk.

We sat, ate warm cookies, drank milk and talked. Rachel asked if I had a girlfriend. I said not at the moment. I gave her the code to my apartment since she will be coming and going for the next two weeks or until they get her a new stove.

I was putting the stuff in the sink. We were standing facing each other talking when she said you are always wearing a robe every time I come over, what's under that robe.

Rachel untied my robe and opened it wide. She said oh wow that's a big fucking cock. She said oh shit I shouldn't have done that; I don't know why I did that shit.

I said its ok you were curious, accidents happen. Rachel said now I can't unsee, your very muscular body and really nice big dick.

I said thanks you have a really amazing body too. Rachel said thank you then she hugged me tight. She said oh wow that is really hard boy. I said sorry your body turns me on.

Rachel said oh wow you are turned on by me, really. I said yeah why is that so hard to believe while still hugging me. She said don't say hard and we both laughed out loud.

She said I didn't think black guys were into me. I said really, you are married, you probably didn't notice guys checking out your big juicy ass, sweet white thighs or big titties.

Rachel said I guess once you're married, you forget about all the stuff to look for when you're dating or looking for a mate to settle down with for the rest of your life.

Rachel said I better stop hugging you before I get even wetter. I said wow, your wet. She said what did you expect with your big hard cock pressed against my vagina.

Rachel said I better go, I said thanks for the cookies. She said your welcome baby. I walked her to the door. She hugged me tight and said oh wow that big thing is still hard as shit.

I said it's not going to go down with your hot ass around. We both laughed and she said bye baby. I said later sexy.

I went to my home office and got some work done then went to bed later. I was asleep when I heard, hello are you up yet, its Rachel. I said sorry I was asleep. She came to my bedroom and said wow you're sleeping in late. I said I worked hard yesterday.

I was under the covers as she sat on my bed in a short white skirt and red panties. I was naked under the covers in the air conditioning of this hot Florida summer.

Rachel yanked the covers off and said time to get up that is when she said oh crap, you are naked and hard as shit again. I said you're wearing a short white skirt and red panties of course I'm hard.

She said oops didn't mean to flash you my red panties. I said its ok I love red panties on a white girl. She said cool, I'm glad you like them.

Rachel said I can't seem to take my eyes off your big fucking dick. I said I don't mind a beautiful woman looking at my hard cock.

Rachel said can I make you breakfast. I said sure and I told her what I wanted. She left and went to the kitchen. I put on a robe and went to the kitchen to have breakfast with Rachel.

I said thanks for breakfast, she said you're welcome stud and I smiled at her. We sat and ate talking like normal. Rachel said I can't stop thinking of your big black cock. I think I'm obsessed with it, can I take a picture of it, is it still hard. I said yeah and sure you can take a picture of my hard cock. I stood up in front of Rachel and she took a ton of pictures of my chocolate stick.

She said cool thank you so much for letting me do that, I better hide these on my phone, so my husband doesn't find it. I said good thinking we don't want him finding another man's cock on his hot wife's phone.

Rachel said tell me about it that's why I store them in a locked folder and deleted them from my pictures. I said that will keep them safe for your pretty blue eyes only.

She said I'm sorry I'm so naughty, kinky and bad, my husband has no idea I'm like this, he thinks I'm a good little girl he married. I said your secret is safe with me.

I said I love a naughty girl, she said I guess that is why we get along so well. Rachel said can I sit on your lap while you eat breakfast. I said sure have a seat. Rachel got up, sat on my lap then said damn this feel so good.

I said your ass feels really good on my cock. Rachel then rubbed my chest saying I love your big muscles, I said thanks horny Rachel.

She got up and said open your robe I want to grind on that big fucking cock. I opened my robe, Rachel lifted up her skirt sat on my cock and started giving me a lap dance. I moaned oh god so good and she said I love your big dick. I massaged her sweet white thighs then I felt up her big tits. She wasn't wearing a bra damn.

Rachel got up and took her panties off. She said I can't take it anymore I need your big fucking cock inside of my white pussy. She kissed the hell out of me.

She stroked my hard cock and slid her married white pussy down my black pole.

Rachel started fucking me with her tight ass pussy, sweet fuck it felt good. Rachel fucked my cock hard and fast. I felt her moisturizing my cock with her pussy cream as she screamed out in pleasure.

I picked her up and took her to the couch with my dick still in her tight pussy. I put her on the couch gently and started fucking her hard. She kissed me as I fucked the shit out of her tight ass pussy.

I said I'm happy your stove broke. Rachel replied me too, I've been wet since you invited me into your apartment. She said one time I saw you at the gym working out, I got so horny I had to leave. I said I never saw you at the gym. She said but I saw you and I had the vapers. I said I'm happy that you are into me, I'm definitely into you.

The next morning, I was asleep when I felt the bed move, Rachel spooned me and started stroking my hard cock. She said good morning lover, time to wake up the horny girl next door needs her daily dose of black cock. I said good morning Rachel, I jumped on her and kissed her before shoving my cock up her wet cunt. She moaned oh big daddy, fuck my tight little pussy with your big fucking cock.

I held her arms down and showed her pussy no mercy. I pounded the shit out of Rachel as she gave of the cream frequently before I filled her up with my warm sperm. I kissed her and said good morning horny Rachel, how are you today?

She said I'm great now that I have had some black in my white pussy. I said I'm glad I can help with that; we were in bed cuddling when she got a call from her sister Randi.

She said oh crap it's my sister Randi. She answered and said Hey sis what's up. They talked for a while then hung up. Rachel said do you know any good hotels around here. I said why, my sister wants to visit, and she can't stay with me. My husband doesn't get along well with my family. I said oh crap that's not good. Rachel said tell me about it.

I said she can stay here, Rachel said really, you are the best lover ever so good to me. I said my pleasure, when is she coming. Rachel said next week, sorry we will have to cool it when she is here. I said its ok, we can fuck like bunnies before and after she comes and goes.

The following week, Rachel brings her sister to my apartment. She said this is a friend of mine who has generously offered you to stay here to avoid my husband.

Randi said thanks for letting me stay. I said my pleasure, I took her things to her room and helped her settle in. I thought damn Randi looks just like her sister. I wonder if she is a horndog like her big sister.

Rachel said guess what they got my stove in early and installed it last night. I said great you must be happy to have a stove again. Rachel said oh yeah very happy. She left Randi and me to our own devices.

Randi was wearing a sexy little dress showing a lot of

cleavage and sweet white thighs. We were talking and I said love your cute summer dress. She said I love the summer; I wear as little as possible. I smiled at her and she smiled back at me.

Nighttime came upon us quickly. Randi got ready for bed and so did I. I was in the kitchen getting some water when Randi came in wearing the smallest tank top that barely covered her melons. I could see half tits and red panties.

Good thing I had on my robe. I left and went to my bedroom. Randi knocked on my door, I said come in Randi. She was wearing a robe this time. I thought good she was covered up. She said I hate sleeping alone would you mind if I shared your bed. I said no problem hop in.

Randi took off her robe to reveal that she was totally naked. I thought wow as she went under the covers. She cuddled up to me and said I hope you don't mind me sleeping naked in your bed. I said no I don't mind, I'm naked too.

Randi cuddled up to me and massaged my chest as we watched the news. She ran her hands all the way down to my hard cock. She said oh my god that's a big cock. I said thank you, Randi. She asked if I liked white girls. I said I like white girls and she said I like black boys.

I said your horny aren't you. She said oh yeah, I'd like a strong black man to mount me and fuck me until he shoots his cream. I kissed Randi and got on top of her. She kissed my neck and said fuck me bid daddy; I want it really bad. I forced my cock into her tight cunt and gave her what she wanted deep.

Randi held my lower back and put her feet on my thighs as I gave her a good fucking, she squealed with pleasure just like her sister. I couldn't believe I was fucking Rachel's sister the first night wow. I bent her over and fucked her harder pulling her blonde hair like I do her sister. Randi loved it and cream me again wow, two already. I pounded the shit out of her and she loved it. Randi said oh my god I love doggie as I wore her pussy out. She squeezed my dick with her last orgasm and I filled her with my warm fresh seed. I smacked her ass and said thanks Randi. She said your welcome, it's the least I can do for you letting me stay. I said my pleasure and she said mine too smiling at me.

We went to sleep satisfied. We woke up and had breakfast. Rachel came over to see her sister. They went out and I hung around my apartment. I spent two weeks banging Rachel's sister like a drum then she left. Rachel was back in my bed and I was happy about it.

After we fucked, she looked sad and I asked her what the problem was and she told me that my mom wants to visit, I have to give up your big wonderful cock again. I said its ok, I don't mind your mom staying here.

When Rachel and her mom showed up. I was surprised at how young her mom looked. Rose hugged me tight and said thanks for letting me stay, sorry we don't get along with Rachel's husband. I said I'm happy to have you here.

We sat and talked. Rose said I'm happy to get away from my husband, he is useless. I said I'm sorry to hear that, she said he has erectile disfunction. So, I'm horny all the time with no relieve.

I hugged her and said I'm sorry to hear that, she said a man hasn't been this close to me in years.

I smiled at her. It was dinner time and Rose dressed up for it. I said why are you all dressed up. Rose said I like to look nice when a handsome gentleman is around maybe I'll get lucking and you will take advantage of me. We both laughed out loud, you are too funny, I said to her.

She said can you zip me up. I said sure, I zipped her up and we sat down to dinner. She spread her sweet white thighs and I saw her white pussy for the first time. I became arouse and she noticed.

She said you like what you see sweetheart. I said your pussy looks inviting and she said it is, that is when she said my parents told me when I was 16 that I can never take a black lover. I said I'm sorry to hear that and she said I've been craving black penis ever since. I said would you like some black penis, Rose.

Rose said fuck yeah, she got up and took my hand, leading us both to her room. She said you better unzip me. I unzipped her dress and it fell to the ground. She was totally naked, I said you're so beautiful Rose. She said yeah right just fuck me please, I haven't had a dick in five years.

Rose jump on the bed and said take me you young stud. I kissed Rose and violated her white pussy properly. Rose said oh wow your cock is huge and very pleasurable. I felt her first orgasm just five strokes in. I kept fucking Rose, she came a few more times as I pounded her.

She held me tight and took all of me. It felt so wrong being inside of Randi and Rachel's mom. But felt so right in the moment. I kissed her and filled her up with my warm seed. Rose said don't take it out, I want to savor this moment for as long as possible. Who knows when I'll get fucked again?

I stayed in Rose until I went soft. She said thanks for

taking care of me. I said my pleasure Rose. Rose and I spend a very romantic week filled with a lot of pleasure together until she unfortunately had to go home.

A month later and Rose called me. I agreed to come to her beach house to give her some birthday cock. I left the out of town sign on my doorbell. I went to Rose's beach house. We hung out then went to her bedroom to make love.

I was fucking Rose balls deep, I moaned and ejaculated inside of Rose when her daughters came into the bedroom and yelled surprise. They both said oh my god mom you're getting some birthday cock. I dismounted their mom's pussy with cream still flowing from my cock.

Rachel said did you just ejaculate inside my mother. I said yeah, I said she wanted birthday cock and I was happy to fuck her on her birthday. Randi said your cock is really big and cream is coming out of it. Rose said thanks for the birthday cock, your dad has erectile dysfunction, I went 5 years with no cock but no more.

Randy and Rachel were in shock with their mouths open from what their mom said and eyes on my cock which became hard again with their pretty blue eyes on it.

The end

www.ingramcontent.com/pod-product-compliance
Lightning Source LLC
LaVergne TN
LVHW020540160826
845677LV00015B/4148

* 9 7 9 8 8 4 7 4 5 7 4 7 7 *